بسم الله الرحمن الرحيم

What Should We Say?

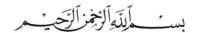

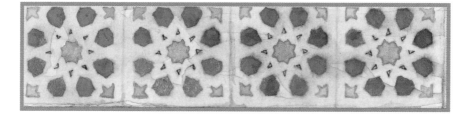

Reprint 2002 and 2005/1426AH

ISBN 0 86037 267 7

MUSLIM CHILDREN'S LIBRARY
WHAT SHOULD WE SAY?
Compiled and explained by: A. R. Kidwai, F. M. D'Oyen

Published by
The Islamic Foundation
Markfield Conference Centre, Ratby Lane, Markfield
Leicestershire, LE67 9SY, United Kingdom
Tel: 01530 244944/5, Fax: 01530 244946
E-mail: info@islamic-foundation.org.uk
publications@islamic-foundation.com
Website: www.islamic-foundation.org.uk

Quran House, PO Box 30611, Nairobi, Kenya

PMB 3193, Kano, Nigeria

بسم الله الرحمن الرحيم

What Should We Say?

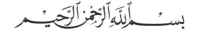

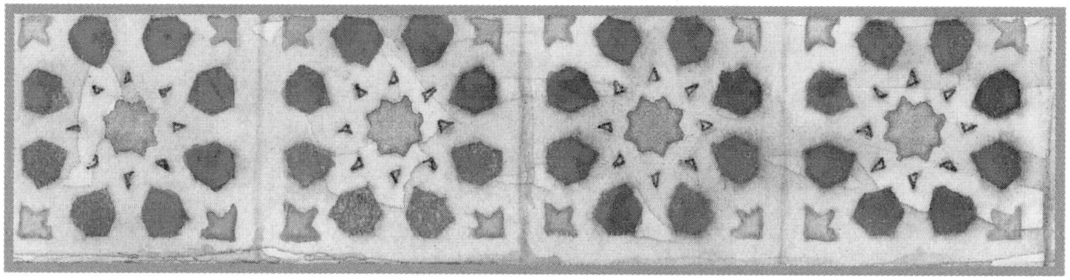

A selection of prayers for daily use

compiled and explained by

A. R. Kidwai & F. M. D'Oyen

illustrated by

Stevan Stratford

THE ISLAMIC FOUNDATION

TRANSLITERATION

Guide to pronouncing Arabic words

For some Arabic vowels and sounds there is no English equivalent. In order to help readers overcome this problem some special marks have been put on certain words in this book.

For example, ā, ī and ū stand for the vowel sounds aa (as in path), ee (as in feet) and oo (as in pool) respectively.

Similarly, the signs (') and (ᶜ) have been used for the Arabic letters *hamza* (as in *Wuḍū'*) and *'ayn* (as in *Kaᶜbah*).

Arabic Alphabet and its English Equivalent

ء	'						
ا	a	د	d	ض	ḍ	ك	k
ب	b	ذ	dh	ط	ṭ	ل	l
ت	t	ر	r	ظ	ẓ	م	m
ث	th	ز	z	ع	ᶜ	ن	n
ج	j	س	s	غ	gh	ه	h
ح	ḥ	ش	sh	ف	f	و	w
خ	kh	ص	ṣ	ق	q	ي	y

What Should We Say?

Transliteration - Guide to pronouncing Arabic words

CONTENTS

A Note to Parents and Teachers

What Should We Say? is a selection of prayers to be used daily by Muslims, both children and adults. These short prayers have been compiled from the Qur'ān and the example of the Prophet Muḥammad ﷺ, and illustrate in a vivid and concrete manner the Islamic principle that encourages a believer to cultivate God-consciousness in all he does throughout his day.

Too often, these prayers are taught to young children by rote without an explanation of their meaning. If an explanation is not given, they may be quickly forgotten by children whose native tongue is not Arabic. It is hoped that by providing the original Arabic text as well as guidelines for pronunciation, a translation into simple English and explanatory notes, children will come to appreciate the meaning of these lovely *duʿā'*, and their faith will be strengthened.

Although it is unlikely that children in middle childhood (7–11 years) will be able to learn these prayers by heart from a book without the guidance of adults, a book can be a useful tool to aid the memory. We suggest that you allow approximately one week for the child to learn each prayer, first discussing and explaining the meaning of the prayer and then practising its correct pronunciation several times, once or twice a day. It may also be useful for the child to copy the prayers into a book of his own, which he may decorate or illustrate as he pleases, or to act out various situations with other children in which the *duʿā'* may be used. As for the second step, which is to get the child to remember to say the prayers at the appropriate time or occasion, the best teaching method is by personal example.

We hope that this simple work will be of service to you in your struggle in the noble cause of guiding children to the remembrance of Allah, the One God, and we welcome any suggestions for improvements.

Dear Reader,

Dhikr, means to remember Allah.

The Qur’ān says that remembering Allah is the greatest and best thing we can do. And our dear Prophet Muḥammad ﷺ encouraged us to try and keep Allah in our minds and hearts at all times.

There are many ways to remember Allah. We can do so by reading the Qur’ān, or by repeating His Beautiful Names. We can also mention Him throughout the day, by saying words such as *‘bismillāh’* (in Allah’s name), *al-ḥamdulillah* (praise be to Allah) and *jazak-Allāh* (may Allah reward you).

This book teaches one kind of remembrance: the short *duʿā’*, or prayers, that the Prophet Muḥammad ﷺ recommended we repeat throughout our day. On the first few pages you will find a list of many short *duʿā’*, which you may have already learnt from your parents, or from the book *What Do We Say?* for younger children. The *duʿā’* in this book are a little longer, but they are easy to learn. Try to learn them by heart, understand what they mean, and put them into practice – doing so can help you be a better Muslim.

May Allah bless you and help you to remember Him always.

Āmīn.

Short *Duᶜā'* for all Occasions

بِسْمِ اللَّهِ

Bismillāh

'In the name of Allah'

We say this when we begin something, such as reciting the Qur'ān, eating, getting into a vehicle, etc. It is also found at the beginning of almost all *sūrahs* of the Qur'ān.

اَلْحَمْدُ لِلَّهِ

Al-ḥamdulillāh

'Praise be to Allah'

We say this to show our gratefulness to Allah. We also say it when we sneeze, in order to thank Allah for relieving us from our discomfort.

يَرْحَمُكَ اللَّهُ

Yarḥamuka-Allāh

'May Allah have mercy on you'

When one Muslim sneezes and says *al-ḥamdulillāh*, the other Muslims present ask Allah to be merciful to him, by saying *yarḥamuka-Allāh,* or *yarḥamukum-Allāh*.

اَلسَّلامُ عَلَيْكُمْ

As-salāmu ᶜAlaykum

'May peace be with you'

This is the greeting we give when we meet other Muslims.

وَعَلَيْكُمُ اَلسَّلامُ

Wa ʿAlaykum as-Salām

'And may peace also be with you'

This is the reply to the greeting of peace, showing our brotherly love and best wishes. We can also return a longer greeting... saying *Wa ʿalaykum as-salām wa raḥmatullāh*, or, *wa ʿalaykum as-salām wa raḥmatullāhi wa barakātuhū.*

فِي أَمَانِ اللَّهِ

Fī Amānillāh

'Go with Allah's protection'

We use this when we say farewell to someone.

مَاشَاءَ اللَّهُ

Māshā' Allāh

'Allah has willed it'

We say this on happy occasions, when hearing good news or when complimenting someone.

إِنْ شَاءَ اللَّهُ

Inshā' Allāh

'If Allah wills'

Whenever we make a promise or an intention to do something in the future, we add *inshā' Allāh*, remembering that we can only do so with Allah's help.

أَسْتَغْفِرُ اللَّهَ

Astaghfirullāh

'I seek Allah's forgiveness'

This is what we say when we feel sorry for something we have thought, said or done.

جَزَاكَ اللَّهُ

Jazāk-Allāh

'May Allah reward you'

When we thank a fellow Muslim for something he has done, we can say *Jazāk-Allāh,* asking Allah to reward him.

أَعُوذُ بِاللَّهِ

Aʿūdhubillāh

'I seek refuge in Allah'

Whether we are afraid, angry or wish to ward off an evil thought, we can seek Allah's help and protection by saying *Aʿūdhubillāh*.

What should we say?

When we get up?

الْحَمْدُ لِلَّهِ الَّذِي أَحْيَانَا بَعْدَ مَا أَمَاتَنَا وَإِلَيْهِ النُّشُورُ.

Al-ḥamdu lillāhil-ladhī aḥyānā baʿda mā amātanā wa ilayhin-nushūr.

'Praise be to Allah, Who revived us to life after making us sleep; and we arise to Him.'

In a way, being asleep is like being dead; we are not aware of what is happening around us when we sleep. Sometimes when people die, we say, 'They have gone to their final resting place.'

Saying this little prayer when we wake up reminds us that it is Allah Who gives us night and day, makes us sleep and wake up. We show our gratitude to Him for giving us another day to live. This prayer also reminds us that just as Allah wakes us up each morning, He will bring us all back to life after death on the Day of Judgement.

What should we say when we go to the toilet?

اللَّهُمَّ إِنِّي أَعُوذُ بِكَ مِنَ الْخُبْثِ وَالْخَبَائِثِ.

Allāhumma innī aʿūdhu-bika minal-khubthi wa'l-khabā'ith.

'O Allah! I seek Your protection against filth and impurities.'

Islam is a religion of purity and cleanliness. When we go to the toilet, we should take care to clean ourselves properly. We should also make sure that our clothes do not become soiled, and we should leave the toilet as clean for the next person as we would like to find it ourselves.

What should we say when we leave the toilet?

غُفْرَانَكَ

Ghufrānak.

('O Allah!) I seek Your forgiveness.'

We ask Allah to forgive us for our mistakes and impurities, and we try to keep ourselves clean in body, mind and soul.

What should we say when we start doing *wuḍū'*?

اللَّهُمَّ اغْفِرْ لِي ذَنْبِي وَوَسِّعْ لِي فِي دَارِي وَبَارِكْ لِي فِي رِزْقِي.

Allāhumma-ghfirlī dhanbī wa-wassi'lī fī dārī wa-bārik lī fī rizqī.

'O Allah! Forgive my sins, give me abundance in my home and bless me in what You have given me.'

The Prophet ﷺ once explained that our sins are washed away when we make *wuḍū'* just as dead leaves fall from a tree when it is shaken, if we take care to make our *wuḍū'* properly and with a sincere intention. As we put aside our work for a few minutes in order to pray, we ask Allah to bless whatever worldly activities we are leaving for His sake.

What should we say when we complete wuḍū'?

أَشْهَدُ أَنْ لاَ إِلَهَ إِلاَّ اللَّهُ وَحْدَهُ لاَ شَرِيكَ لَهُ وأَشْهَدُ أَنَّ مُحَمَّداً
عَبْدُهُ وَرَسُولُهُ. اَللَّهُمَّ اجْعَلْنِي مِنَ التَّوَّابِينَ وَاجْعَلْنِي مِنَ الْمُتَطَهِّرِينَ.

Ash-hadu an-lā-ilāha illal-lāhu waḥdahū lā-sharīka lahū wa-ash-hadu anna Muḥammadan ʿabduhū wa-rasūluh. Allāhumma-jʿalnī minat-tawwābīn wajʿalnī minal-mutaṭahhirīn.

'I witness that there is no god but Allah (the One God). He is One and has no partner. And I witness that Muḥammad is His servant and Messenger.

O Allah! Make me one of the people who repent often (for their sins) and keep themselves pure.'

We make our *wuḍū'* complete by renewing our testimony of faith in Allah Who has given us the priceless gift of the guidance of Islam, and His Messenger Muḥammad ﷺ who taught us how to live.

What should we say when we get dressed?

اَلْحَمْدُ لِلَّهِ الَّذِي كَسَانِي مَا أُوَارِي بِهِ عَوْرَتِي وَأَتَجَمَّلُ بِهِ فِي حَيَاتِي.

Al-ḥamdulillāhil-ladhī kasānī mā uwārī bihī ʿawratī wa-atajammalu bihī fī ḥayātī.

'Praise be to Allah Who has given me clothing with which I cover my body and adorn myself in life.'

Clothing not only covers our nakedness from the view of others and protects us from the heat and cold, rain and wind, but also gives us a beautiful and dignified appearance. We thank Allah for each new article of clothing which we receive, as well as the person who has given it to us.

What should we say when we look in the mirror?

اَلْحَمْدُ لِلَّهِ. اَللَّهُمَّ حَسِّنْ خُلُقِي كَمَا حَسَّنْتَ خَلْقِي.

Alḥamdulillāh. Allāhumma ḥassin khuluqī kamā ḥassanta khalqī.

'Praise be to Allah. O Allah, just as You have created my body in an excellent form, please make my character excellent as well.'

Unlike people, Allah does not judge us by our bodies, but by our hearts. Regardless of how we look, we should always remember it is our character, manners and habits which are most important.

What should we say when we start eating?

بِسْمِ اللّٰهِ (وَعَلَى بَرَكَةِ اللّٰهِ).

Bismillāh [wa ʿalā barakatil-lāh].

'In the name of Allah [and with Allah's blessing].'

There are a number of different *duʿā'* we can say as a grace at meals. This one, which is short and simple, reminds us that our food comes from Allah, and is a great blessing from Him.

What should we say when we break our fast?

اَللّٰهُمَّ لَكَ صُمْتُ وَبِكَ آمَنْتُ وَعَلَى رِزْقِكَ أَفْطَرْتُ، فَاغْفِرْ لِي.

Allāhumma laka ṣumtu wa-bika āmantu waʿalā rizqika afṭartu faghfirlī.

'O Allah, I have fasted for You, I believe in You, and I am breaking my fast with what You have provided for me, so forgive me.'

If we are fasting, it is *sunnah* to say this additional supplication before saying *bismillāh*.

What should we say if we forget *Bismillāh* at the beginning of a meal?

بِسْمِ اللَّهِ أَوَّلَهُ وَآخِرَهُ.

Bismillāhi awwalahū wa-ākhirahū.

'In Allah's name at the beginning and at the end.'

Sometimes we are in such a hurry to eat that we forget to mention Allah's name at the beginning of the meal. This simple prayer eases our conscience and allows us to enjoy the rest of our meal with the full blessings of Allah.

What should we say when we finish eating?

اَلْحَمْدُ لِلَّهِ الَّذِي أَطْعَمَنَا وَسَقَانَا وَجَعَلَنَا مِنَ الْمُسْلِمِينَ.

Al-ḥamdulillāhil-ladhī aṭʿamanā wa saqānā wa jaʿalanā minal-muslimīn.

'Praise be to Allah Who has given us food and drink and made us Muslims.'

Even as we begin our meal with Allah's name, we should remember to thank Him for our food and drink and the blessings of Islam when we finish eating.

What should we say when we start to recite the Holy Qur'ān?

أَعُوذُ بِاللَّهِ مِنَ الشَّيْطَانِ الرَّجِيمِ، بِسْمِ اللَّهِ الرَّحْمَانِ الرَّحِيمِ.

Aʿūdhu billāhi minash-shayṭānir-rajīm, bismillāhir-raḥmānir-raḥīm.

'I seek Allah's protection from the cursed Satan. (I begin) in the name of Allah, the Most Compassionate, Most Merciful.'

Allah tells us in the Qur'ān that we should seek His protection from Satan before beginning our recitation of the blessed Qur'ān. This helps us focus our attention and prevents us from becoming distracted, or thinking bad thoughts. And then we begin by saying *bismillāh*, as we do at the start of all important things.

What should we say when we leave the house?

بِسْمِ اللَّهِ، تَوَكَّلْتُ عَلَى اللَّهِ، وَلاَ حَوْلَ وَلاَ قُوَّةَ إلاَّ بِاللَّهِ.

Bismillāh, tawakkaltu ʿalallāh, wa lā ḥawla wa lā quwwata illā-billāh.

'In the name of Allah (I depart), placing my trust in Allah. There is no power or strength except in Allah.'

Saying this prayer shows that we rely on Allah to protect us from all harm whenever we leave our home.

What should we say when we travel by car, bus or by other means of transport?

سُبْحَانَ الَّذِي سَخَّرَ لَنَا هذَا وَمَا كُنَّا لَهُ مُقْرِنِينَ وَإِنَّا إِلَى رَبِّنَا لَمُنْقَلِبُونَ.

Subḥānal-ladhī sakhkhara lanā hādhā wa mā kunnā lahū muqrinīn wa innā ilā rabbinā la-munqalibūn.

'Glory be to the One Who has made it possible for us to master this (car, animal, etc.) for our own needs, for we would never be able to accomplish it on our own. And we will surely return to our Lord (in the end).'

One of Allah's wonders is that He has created so many ways for us to travel and care for our needs. Through the gift of the human mind, people have discovered a great variety of transport: donkey, horse, camel, bicycle, motorcycle, car, bus, train, tram, canoe, ship, hovercraft, hot air balloon, airplane and even spaceship! Without the gift of intelligence, without the animals that can be trained to help us, and without the many materials that the earth provides, we would be left to make our way about on our own two feet! This prayer reminds us to be grateful for these favours, and also lets us consider the fact that, at the end of our life's journey, we will return to Allah, our Maker.

What should we say when we hear the Adhān?

اَللَّهُمَّ رَبَّ هَذِهِ الدَّعْوَةِ التَّامَّةِ وَالصَّلاَةِ الْقَائِمَةِ آتِ مُحَمَّداً اَلْوَسِيلَةَ
والْفَضِيلَةَ وَابْعَثْهُ مَقَاماً مَحْمُوداً الَّذِي وَعَدْتَهُ.

Allāhumma rabba hādhihid-daᶜwatit-tāmmati waṣ-ṣalātil-qā'imati āti Muḥammadan-il-wasīlata wal-faḍīlata wabᶜathhu maqāmam maḥmūdan-il-ladhī waᶜadtahū.

'O Allah! Lord of this perfect call (to prayer) and of the prayer about to be offered, make Muḥammad the means (of approach to You on the Day of Judgement), and favour him with excellence, and raise him to the high and praiseworthy position which You have promised him.'

The Prophet ﷺ taught us that Allah will not reject a *duᶜā'* made between the time of the first and second calls to prayer (the *adhān* and the *iqāmah*). In order to express thanks to our beloved Prophet ﷺ, we first ask Allah to honour him; then we may follow this with any other personal prayer of our choice.

What should we say when we enter a mosque?

اَللَّهُمَّ افْتَحْ لِي أَبْوَابَ رَحْمَتِكَ.

Allāhumma-iftaḥ lī abwāba raḥmatik.

'O Allah! Open for me the gates of Your mercy!'

We go to the mosque to worship Allah, and during our worship we draw nearer to Allah. Saying this prayer reminds us of Allah's great kindness and mercy. If we have been thinking of other things, it helps us turn our attention towards Him as we enter His house of worship.

What should we say when we mention or hear the Prophet's name?

صَلَّى اللَّهُ عَلَيْهِ وَسَلَّمَ.

Ṣallallāhu ʿalayhi wasallam.

'May Allah bless him and grant him peace.'

The Prophet Muḥammad ﷺ taught, 'Pray for me, for truly your prayers reach me wherever you are,' and, 'Whoever asks Allah to bless me once will be blessed by Allah ten times.'

What should we say when we leave a mosque?

اَللَّهُمَّ إِنِّي أَسْأَلُكَ مِنْ فَضْلِكَ.

Allāhumma innī as'aluka min faḍlik.

'O Allah! I seek Your favour.'

Even as we ask for Allah's mercy as we enter the mosque, we seek His blessing for our worldly activities as we depart.

What should we say when we study?

رَبِّ زِدْنِي عِلْماً.

Rabbi zidnī ʿilmā.

'O Lord! Increase me in knowledge.'

This short prayer from the Qur'ān teaches us the great value Islam places on knowledge and learning. We should always do our best to learn as much useful knowledge as we can, and put into practice what we have learnt.

What should we say when we face a problem?

حَسْبُنَا اللَّهُ وَنِعْمَ الْوَكِيلُ.

Ḥasbunallāhu wa niʿmal-wakīl.

'Allah is enough for us, and He is the best Guardian.'

Saying this prayer when we are in difficulties reminds us to turn to Allah for help, for He has power over all things. It also strengthens our faith and courage so that we can face our troubles calmly.

What should we say when we are angry?

أَعُوذُ بِاللَّهِ مِنَ الشَّيْطَانِ الرَّجِيمِ.

Aʿūdhu billāhi minash-shayṭānir-rajīm.

'I seek Allah's protection from the cursed Satan.'

The Prophet ﷺ said that anger is from Satan, and that Satan likes to see us get angry. Other things we can do to control our anger is to make *wuḍū'*, to sit down if we are standing, and to lie down if we are sitting.

What should we say when we visit someone who is sick?

لاَ بَأسَ، طَهُوراً إِنْ شَاءَ اللَّهُ.

Lā ba'sa ṭahūran inshā'Allāh.

'Never mind (do not worry); it will purify you (from your sins), Allah-willing.'

Sick people sometimes worry that they might not get better. Even when a person is very ill, the Prophet ﷺ advised us to try and cheer him up. We can remind him that every illness will purify a Muslim of some of his sins. This is a comforting thought for a sincere believer.

What should we say when we hear of someone's death?

إِنَّا لِلَّهِ وَإِنَّا إِلَيْهِ رَاجِعُونَ.

Innā lillāhi wa innā ilayhi rājiʿūn.

'We belong to Allah and we will return to Him.'

This short prayer tells us that we all must die one day, and return to our Maker.

What should we say when we pass by a graveyard?

اَلسَّلَامُ عَلَيْكُمْ يَا أَهْلَ الْقُبُورِ، يَغْفِرُ اللَّهُ لَنَا
وَلَكُمْ، أَنْتُمُ السَّابِقُونَ وَنَحْنُ اللَّاحِقُونَ.

As-salāmu ʿalaykum yā ahlal-qubūr, yaghfirullāhu lanā wa-lakum, antumus-sābiqūna wa naḥnul-lāḥiqūn.

'Peace be with you, O people of the graves! May Allah forgive you and us. You were the first (to die) and we will follow you (sooner or later).'

Saying this prayer reminds us that death will come to us all, and we should prepare for it by making the most of every day of our lives.

What should we say when we return home from a journey?

آيِبُونَ تَائِبُونَ عَابِدُونَ لِرَبِّنَا حَامِدُونَ.

Āyibūna tā'ibūna ʿābidūna li-rabbinā ḥāmidūn.

'(We) return, repenting, worshipping, and praising our Lord.'

When we reach the safety and comfort of home after a long journey, we show our gratitude to Allah, repent of any sins we may have committed during our travels and praise Him for bringing us to our loved ones once again. We also greet our family by saying *as-salāmu ʿalaykum* (peace be with you).

What should we say when we go to bed?

بِاسْمِكَ اَللَّهُمَّ أمُوتُ وَأحْيَا .

Bismik-Allāhumma amūtu wa aḥyā.

'O Allah, in Your name I live and die.'

Another Duʿā':

بِاسْمِكَ رَبِّي وَضَعْتُ جَنْبِي وَبِكَ أرْفَعُهُ، إِنْ أمْسَكْتَ نَفْسِي
فَارْحَمْهَا ، وَإِنْ أرْسَلْتَهَا فَاحْفَظْهَا بِمَا تَحْفَظُ بِهِ عِبَادَكَ الصَّالِحِينَ.

Bismika rabbī waḍaʿtu janbī wa bika arfaʿuhu, in amsakta nafsī farḥamhā, wa in arsaltahā faḥfaẓhā bimā taḥfaẓu bihī ʿibādak-aṣ-ṣāliḥīn.

'In Your name, my Lord, I lay myself down, and in Your name I raise myself. If You keep hold of my soul (when I sleep), then have mercy on it. And if You send it back (to live another day), then protect it as You protect Your pious servants.'

With this prayer, we ask Allah to safeguard our souls in life and death. The Prophet ﷺ also used to recite *Sūrahs al-Ikhlāṣ, al-Falaq* and *al-Nās* before he went to sleep, and would wipe his hands over the front of his body when he had finished.

What should we say after a nightmare or an unpleasant dream?

أَعُوذُ بِكَلِمَاتِ اللَّهِ التَّامَّةِ مِنْ غَضَبِهِ وَعِقَابِهِ
وَشَرِّ عِبَادِهِ، وَمِنْ هَمَزَاتِ الشَّيَاطِينِ وَأَنْ يَحْضُرُونَ.

Aʿūdhu bi kalimātil-lāhit-tāmmāti min ghaḍabihī wa ʿiqābihī,
wa sharri ʿibādihī wa min hamazātish-shayāṭīni wa an-yaḥḍurūn.

'I seek refuge in the perfect words of Allah from His anger and His punishment, from the evil of His servants, and from the whispering of devils and from their coming near to me.'

Whenever we are in some kind of trouble or facing a crisis, we should always turn to Allah for help. This short prayer is recommended after a nightmare as well as on other occasions.

A prayer for all occasions

اَللَّهُمَّ إِنِّي أَسْأَلُكَ فِعْلَ الْخَيْرَاتِ وَتَرْكَ الْمُنْكَرَاتِ، وَحُبَّ الْمَسَاكِينِ، وَأَنْ تَغْفِرَ لِي
وَتَرْحَمْنِي ... أَسْأَلُكَ حُبَّكَ وَحُبَّ مَنْ يُحِبُّكَ، وَحُبَّ كُلِّ عَمَلٍ يُقَرِّبُ إِلَى حُبِّكَ.

Allāhumma innī as'aluka fiʿlal-khayrāt wa-tarkal-munkarat, wa ḥubbal-masākīn, wa-an taghfiralī wa-tarḥamnī ... As'aluka ḥubbaka wa ḥubba man-yuḥibbuka, wa-ḥubba kulli ʿamalin yuqarribu ilā ḥubbik.

'O Allah, I ask You to help me do what is good and leave what is bad, and to have love for the poor and needy, and I ask You to forgive me and have mercy on me ... I ask You for Your love, and for the love of those who love You, and for the love of deeds that will draw me near to Your love.'

This is a lovely example of one of the comprehensive prayers taught by the Prophet Muḥammad ﷺ, covering many situations in very few words. It shows us how to ask for Allah's mercy, forgiveness and guidance and reminds us of the concern we should have for those less fortunate than ourselves. It also teaches us that one of the best ways to earn Allah's pleasure is by striving to do good deeds and desiring to be in the company of those who do good deeds, and by trying to imitate those good people.

Prayers from the Holy Qur'ān for Everyday Use

رَبَّنَا لاَ تُزِغْ قُلُوبَنَا بَعْدَ إِذْ هَدَيْتَنَا ، وَهَبْ لَنَا
مِنْ لَّدُنْكَ رَحْمَةً إِنَّكَ أَنْتَ الْوَهَّابُ.

Rabbanā lā-tuzigh qulūbanā baʿda idh-hadaytanā wa-hab lanā mil-ladunka raḥmatan, innaka antal-wahhāb.

(a) 'Our Lord, do not make our hearts go astray after You have guided us, and grant us mercy from Yourself. You grant mercy without measure.'

(Āl ʿImrān 3: 8)

لاَ إِلَهَ إِلاَّ أَنْتَ سُبْحَانَكَ
إِنِّي كُنْتُ مِنَ الظَّالِمِينَ.

Lā ilāha illā anta, subḥānaka innī kuntu minaẓ-ẓālimīn.

(b) 'There is no god but You. Glory be to You! I have done wrong.'

(Al-Anbiyā' 21: 87)

This was the prayer of the Prophet Yūnus ﷺ (Jonah) while he was inside the belly of the great fish. He admitted his fault, and Allah saved him.

رَبَّنَا إِنَّنَا آمَنَّا فَاغْفِرْ لَنَا ذُنُوبَنَا
وَقِنَا عَذَابَ النَّارِ.

Rabbanā innanā āmannā faghfir-lanā dhunūbanā wa-qinā ʿadhāban-nār.

(c) 'Our Lord, surely we believe! So forgive us our sins and save us from the punishment of the Hellfire!'

(Āl ʿImrān 3: 16)

رَبِّ اشْرَحْ لِي صَدْرِي وَيَسِّرْ لِي أمْرِي
وَاحْلُلْ عُقْدَةً مِنْ لِسَانِي يَفْقَهُوا قَوْلِي.

Rabbishraḥ-lī ṣadrī wa-yassirlī amrī waḥlul ʿuqdatan-mil-lisānī yafqahū qawlī.

(d) 'My Lord, open my breast for me, and make my task easy, and take away my handicap in speaking, so that they may understand what I say.'

(Ṭā Hā 20: 25–28)

This was the prayer the Prophet Mūsā ﷷ (Moses) made when Allah commanded him to approach the Pharaoh of Egypt. It is said that Mūsā ﷷ had a speech problem which made it difficult for some people to understand him, and that Allah removed his handicap after he made this *duʿā*'.

رَبَّنَا مَا خَلَقْتَ هَذَا بَاطِلاً، سُبْحَانَكَ فَقِنَا عَذَابَ النَّارِ.

Rabbanā mā-khalaqta hādhā bāṭilan, subḥānaka fa-qinā ʿadhāban-nār.

(e) 'Our Lord, You have not created (all) this in vain. Glory be to You! Protect us from the punishment of the Hellfire.'

(Āl ʿImrān 3: 191)

رَبَّنَا آتِنَا فِي الدُّنْيَا حَسَنَةً وَفِي الآخِرَةِ حَسَنَةً وَقِنَا عَذَابَ النَّارِ.

Rabbanā ātinā fid-dunyā ḥasanatan wa-fil-ākhirati ḥasanatan wa-qinā ʿadhāban-nār.

(f) 'Our Lord, give us (the best) of this world and (the best) of the Life to Come, and protect us from the Hellfire!'

(Al-Baqarah 2: 201)

رَبَّنَا اغْفِرْ لِي وَلِوَالِدَيَّ وَلِلْمُؤْمِنِينَ يَوْمَ يَقُومُ الْحِسَابُ.

Rabbanaghfirlī wa-liwālidayya walil-mu'minīna yawma yaqūmul-ḥisāb.

(g) 'My Lord, forgivc mc and my parents and all the believers on the Day of Judgement!'

(Ibrāhīm 14: 41)

رَبِّ ارْحَمْهُمَا كَمَا رَبَّيَانِي صَغِيراً.

Rabbirḥamhumā kamā rabbayānī ṣaghīrā.

(h) 'My Lord, have mercy on both of them (my parents), as they did care for me when I was little.'

(Al-Isrā' 17: 24)

...فَاطِرَ ٱلسَّمَٰوَٰتِ وَٱلْأَرْضِ أَنتَ وَلِىِّۦ فِى ٱلدُّنْيَا وَٱلْءَاخِرَةِ ۖ
تَوَفَّنِى مُسْلِمًا وَأَلْحِقْنِى بِٱلصَّٰلِحِينَ ﴿١٠١﴾

Fāṭira s-samāwāti wal-arḍi anta waliyyi fi d-dunyā wal-ākhira tawaffanī musliman wa-alḥiqnī biṣ-ṣaliḥin.

(i) O Originator of the heavens and the earth! Be my Protecting Guardian in this life and in the Hereafter. Make me die as a Muslim and join me with the pious ones.

(Yūsuf 12:101)

...رَّبِّ زِدْنِى عِلْمًا ﴿١١٤﴾

Rabbizidnī ʿilman.

(j) O my Lord! Increase me in knowledge.

(Ṭa Hā 20:114)

...رَبِّ أَوْزِعْنِىٓ أَنْ أَشْكُرَ نِعْمَتَكَ ٱلَّتِىٓ أَنْعَمْتَ عَلَىَّ وَعَلَىٰ وَٰلِدَىَّ وَأَنْ أَعْمَلَ
صَـٰلِحًا تَرْضَىٰهُ وَأَدْخِلْنِى بِرَحْمَتِكَ فِى عِبَادِكَ ٱلصَّـٰلِحِينَ ﴿١٩﴾

Rabbi awzi'nī an ashkura ni'matakal-latī an'amta 'alayya wa-'alā wālidayya wa-an a'mala ṣāliḥan tarḍāhu wa-adkhilnī bi-raḥmatika fī 'ibādika ṣ-ṣāliḥīna.

(k) O my Lord! Enable me to thank You for Your favours to me and my parents and to do such good deeds as please You. By Your mercy include me among Your righteous servants.

(al-Naml 27:19)

...رَبِّ إِنِّى لِمَآ أَنزَلْتَ إِلَىَّ مِنْ خَيْرٍ فَقِيرٌ ﴿٢٤﴾

Rabbi innī limā anzalta ilayya min khayrin faqīr.

(l) O my Lord! I am in need of any good which You may send to me.

(al-Qaṣaṣ 28:24)

GLOSSARY OF ISLAMIC TERMS

Allāh	the Arabic name for the One God.
Adhān	the call to prayer, which is announced from the mosque five times a day to summon the faithful.
Dhikr	'the remembrance' (of God); commonly used to refer to the prayerful repetition of certain recommended phrases.
Duʿā'	supplicatory prayer (in contrast to *salah*, the ritual prayer which has specific positions and conditions).
Iqāmah	a shortened version of the call to prayer, recited to signal that the prayer is to begin.
Qur'ān	God's final Book of revelation; the Holy Book of the Muslims.
Sunnah	literally 'tradition', or 'custom'; refers to the blessed example of the Prophet Muḥammad (peace and blessings be upon him) and his way of life.
Sūrah	literally 'wall'; a 'chapter' of the Qur'ān, more similar to an epistle than a chapter in the English sense of the word.
Sūrahs al-Ikhlāṣ, al-Falaq and an-Nās	the last three chapters of the Qur'ān, which are recited for a variety of purposes. The first contains the definitive statement on the Oneness of God *(tawḥid)*, and the second two are a formula to seek Divine protection from evil, envy, trouble and illness in any form.
Wuḍū'	ritual ablution; the washing of the face, hands, arms and feet before prayer and other acts of worship.